Join Marley on a journey to embrace her emotions

Join Marley as she discovers that intense feelings are not negative. She learns that her emotions simply require a bit of love, a deep breath, and someone who truly understands. With her Mama's guidance, Marley uncovers how to identify her feelings, soothe her heart, and take pride in every emotion she experiences.

**Ideal for young children,
this gentle and empowering tale helps children:**

Understand their emotions
Learn simple calming techniques
Feel seen, supported, and empowered

This book belongs to:

____

Marley's Big, Bigger, and Biggest Feelings

Written By
Lindsay Marie

Acknowledgement and Special Thanks

I would like to express my heartfelt appreciation to my talented illustrator, Tayyaba Rasheed, for beautifully bringing this story and Marley to life. Additionally, I want to thank my three wonderful daughters, whose inspiration sparked my creativity in creating Marley. I love you, girls, and I hope you find joy in this book.

Some days, Marley's feelings are small like an ant.
On other days, they are BIG, BIGGER, and BIGGEST.

BIG
BIGGER
BIGGEST

"What's going on in there?" Mama asked, tapping on Marley's chest.
"In here?" Marley asked.
"In there," Mama nodded, smiling.
"That's where your feelings live."

Mama said, "We all have feelings that come in many different sizes. Some are big, and some are small."

Marley thought about the many feelings she had.

smiling

bored

mad

laughing

tired

scared

Sometimes, Marley's feelings were BIG.
Big like a lion's ROAR when she is mad.
ROAR

Big like a **BOOMING** drum when she is scared.

But then, sometimes, her feelings got...
BIGGER than her.
So big, she didn't know what to do with them.
They made her YELL.
They made her SCREAM.

They made her SMILE.
And sometimes, they even
made her laugh.

And sometimes, they were the BIGGEST.
Biggest like a FLOOD when she cried.
A B C
A

Biggest like a ROCKET SHIP when she got excited!

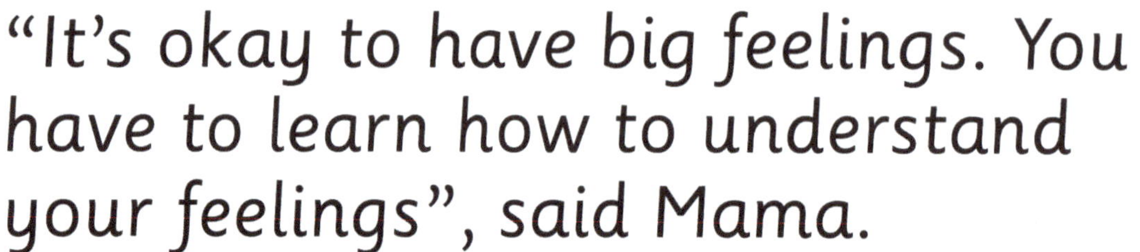

"It's okay to have big feelings. You have to learn how to understand your feelings", said Mama.

"Like this," Mama said. "Let's try"
Breathe in like you're smelling a flower.
Blow out like you're blowing a bubble.

Mama said, "Or you can count to 10."
Marley closes her eyes and counts to 10.
"1 2 3 4 5 6 7 8 9 10"

"Let's name some feeling," Mama said

Mad
Sad
Silly
Scared
Happy
Excited
Lonely
Shy
Proud
Loved
Frustration
Confusion

Now, when your feelings come to visit,
Marley waves and says,
     "Hello, Big Feeling. I see you."
She takes a breath and she lets it out when it's time.

Marley still has big, bigger, and biggest feelings.
And that's okay.
Because now she knows how to take care of them with a breath,
and Mama's love.
She may be small...
but her heart is big enough for every feeling inside.

Activity 1: Your Turn!
What big feelings do you have today?
Draw them.
Name them.
Talk about them with someone you love.

Activity 2:
Write down some ways you deal with your feelings.